A. H. Benjamin "Oh, No," said Elephant

With pictures by Alireza Goldouzian

minedition

"Let's play hide-and-seek!" said everybody.
"Oh, no," said Elephant.
"I'm not good at that."
But he tried.

"I can see you!" said Monkey.

"There you are!"
said Leopard.

"I've found you!" said Zebra.

It was hard for Elephant to hide.
He was too big.

"Let's play leap-frog!" said Leopard.

"Oh, no," said Elephant.
"I'm not good at that."
But he wanted to.

"You'll squash me!" said Monkey

"You'll flatten me!"
said Leopard.
"You'll crush me!"
said Zebra.

And nobody could jump over Elephant, either.
He was too tall.

"Let's jump rope!"
said Monkey.
"Oh, no," said Elephant.
"I'm not good at that."

But he did his best.

"You're useless!"
said Monkey.

"You're foolish!"
said Leopard.

"You're terrible!" said Zebra.

Even when Elephant tried
to jump alone he couldn't.
He was too clumsy.

"Let's play hopscotch!"
said Zebra.
"Oh, no," said Elephant.
"I'm not good at that."

But he gave it a try.

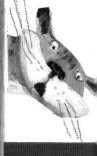

"Missed!"
said Monkey.

"Wrong
square!"
said Leopard.

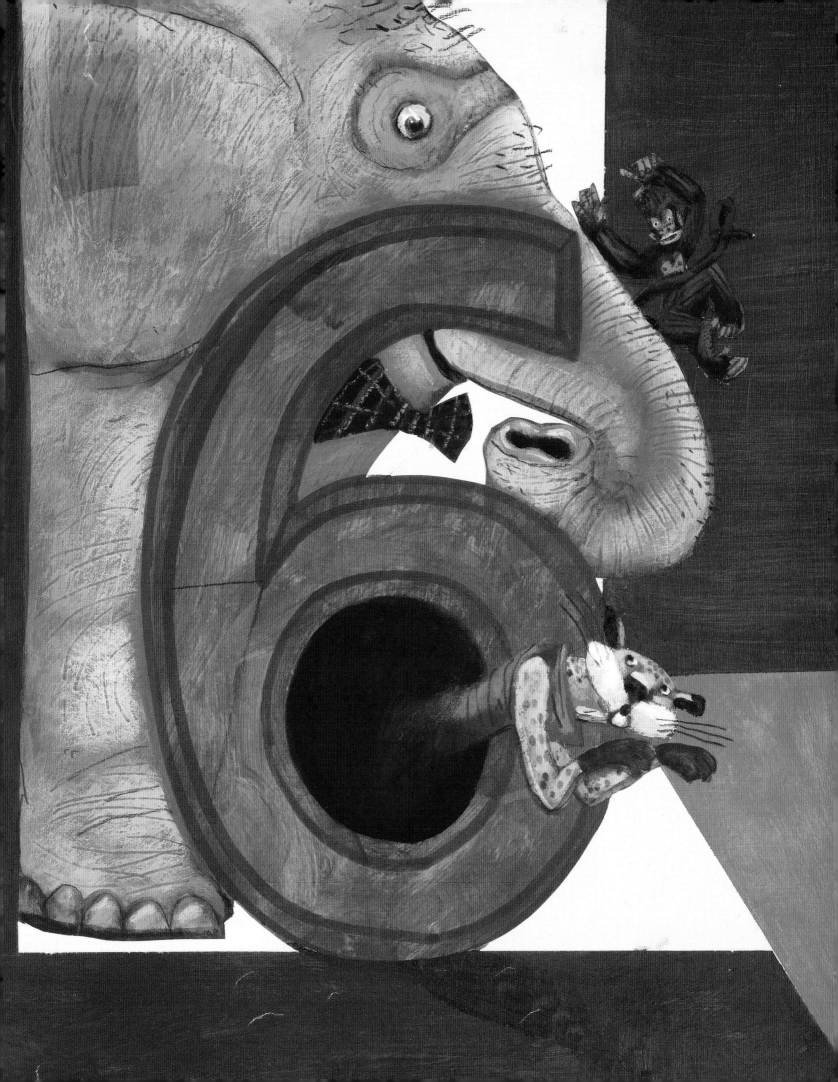

"You're out!" said Zebra.
Elephant couldn't hop at all.
He was too heavy.

"Let's play tag!" said Leopard.
"Oh, no," said Elephant.
"I'm not good at that."
But he didn't mind playing.

"Got your nose!" said Monkey.

"Got your tail!" said Leopard.

"Got your ear!" said Zebra. Elephant was easily tagged. He was too slow.

"What shall we play next?" asked Zebra.
"Tug-of-war!" said Elephant.

"Oh, no," said Monkey, Leopard and Zebra. "We're not good at that."

But it was only fair.

"Pull!" said Monkey.
"Harder!" said Leopard.
"Keep going!" said Zebra.

But they could not beat Elephant.
He was too strong!

"I win!" said Elephant.
"Let's play again!"

"Oh, no," said everybody.

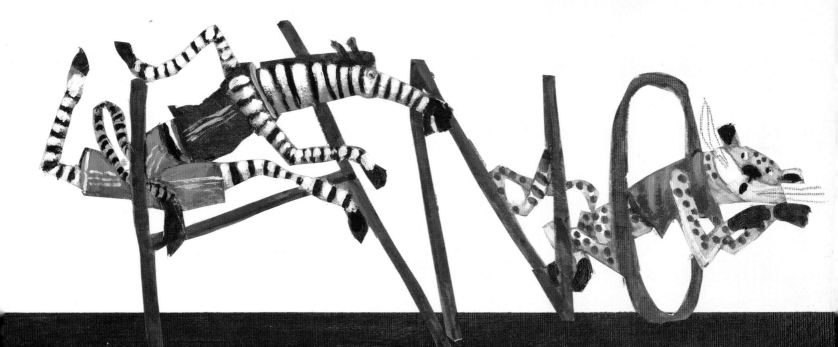

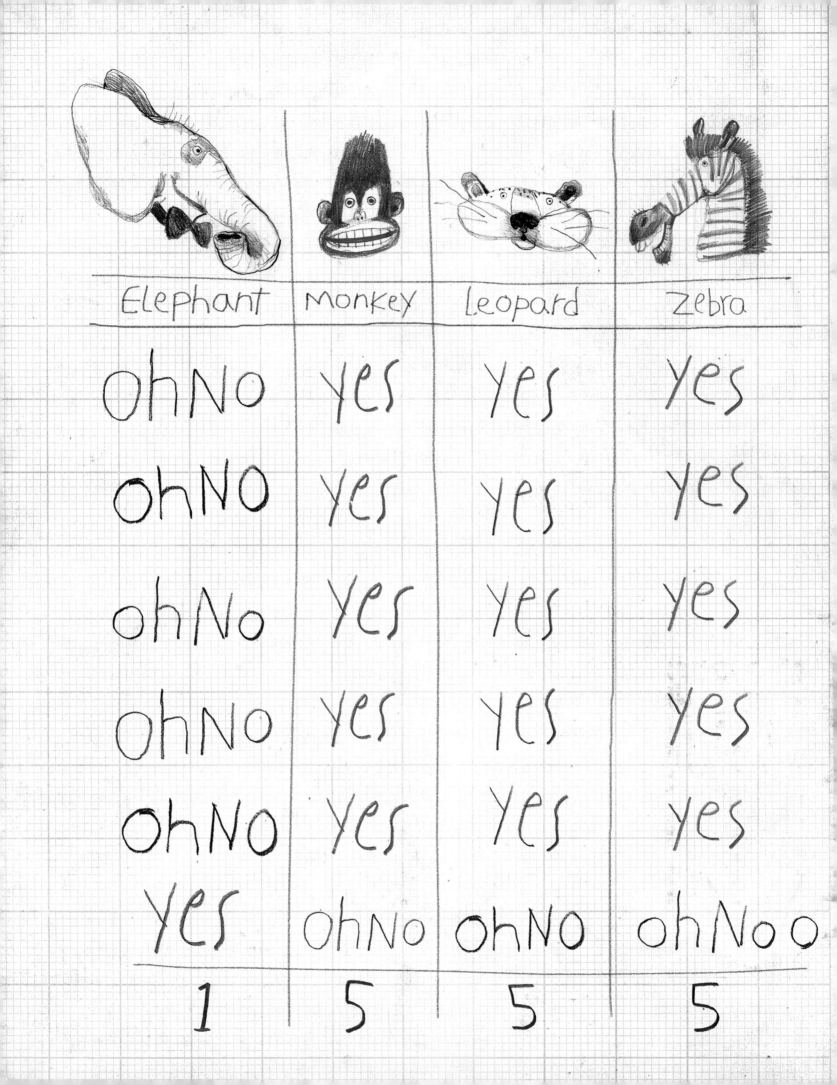

Elephant	Monkey	Leopard	Zebra
OhNo	Yes	Yes	Yes
OhNO	Yes	Yes	Yes
OhNo	Yes	Yes	Yes
OhNO	Yes	Yes	Yes
OhNO	Yes	Yes	Yes
Yes	OhNo	OhNO	OhNoo
1	5	5	5